Big Ben
A Little Known Story

Written and Illustrated by

Mark Loyd

Too FUN! Publishing
Vashon Island, Washington

Dedicated to Londoners — all over the world!

Thank you to:

Therese Kelly Johnson
Devin Johnson, Jennifer Johnson

London research courtesy of the Dean and Chapter of Westminster,
The Library, Westminster Abby - Christine Reynolds,
Rector's Secretary, St. Margaret's Church - Pamela Carrington,
British Consulate, Seattle - Kate Colclough

Kathy Christiansen, Kiki Holbrook, Beverly Kelly,
Linda Kitson, Sally Knutson, Don Johnson, Helen Johnson,
Kate Kaemerle, Chris Lee, George Lee, Sheila Moore, Helen Phillips,
Liesbet Trappenburg, Sharon Waldo and Aunt Davy Werner

In Memory of Jim Kelly

Library of Congress Cataloging in Publication Data

Loyd, Mark
  Big Ben – A Little Known Story

  Summary: A little church mouse takes you on a magical Christmas Eve adventure that
    changes the lives of mice and people of London.

LCCN 2005909172
ISBN 0-9773317-1-7 HBKAP
Copyright © 2006 by Mark Loyd

Printed in Korea

Big Ben
A Little Known Story

TooFUN!
publishing

Vashon Island, Washington

On a cold and foggy winter night, long, long ago, when gas lamps lit the streets, a brave little mouse changed forever the lives of all the mice and people in London.

It was Christmas Eve; families were having fun — enjoying their celebrations. Children were too excited to sleep, knowing Father Christmas — some also call him Santa Claus — would be bringing presents that very night!

Everyone was excited, except for the mice. Christmas Eve was just another day for mice, you know. Oh, goodness, you don't know! I forgot to introduce myself. I'm the Church Mouse Elder. I live with other mice at St. Margaret's Church, next to Westminster Abbey, close to the Parliament Clock Tower.

Well, to get back to my story, Benjamin Mouse, many called him Little Ben, was different. He never quite fit in.

A mouse at St. Margaret's Church had to be quick at gathering food. Ben's big feet would sometimes trip him up. The other church mice often made fun of Little Ben. He wasn't fast at collecting food and he spent too much time daydreaming.

Little Ben sat on a stain glass window ledge, daydreaming once again, wishing mice had more time during the holidays to decorate trees or tell Father Christmas their wishes. *Mice spend too much time scurrying about for food. It isn't much fun,* he thought.

Deep in his heart, he knew that life could be so much more! Jumping down from the ledge, he made a wish to one day have time to decorate a tree and maybe even meet Father Christmas.

Why should I wait another day? he
thought. His eyes got bigger, his heart
pounded with excitement; he knew what
he needed to do. Little Ben stood tall
on a church pew, arms stretched out,
and shouted, "This Christmas will be
different, I will find a way to have fun!"

Determined, he scurried about in search
of a way to escape. Little Ben spotted a
narrow crack in the stone-and-mortar
wall; he drew in his stomach, held his
breath and squeezed through.

When he finally reached the outside, it was dark and blustery cold. Everything wore a blanket of snow. The wind was howling and blowing icy snowflakes that stung Ben's nose and ears, causing him to shiver. Out the corner of his eye, he noticed a warm glow of light near the clock tower, so he pushed on.

The tower was very tall and impressive, especially to a tiny mouse like Little Ben. He looked upward, his eyes following higher and higher, until they reached the ice-covered clock face. In fact, Ben looked up so far, he lost his balance and fell backwards into the snow. He picked himself up, shook off the snow, and continued toward that warm, glowing light. It was coming from under a door.

Maybe if I went inside, I could get warm, Ben thought to himself.

Little Ben peeked through the crack under the door. An old man sat alone in a wooden chair, at a table. He looked so sad — but why? Aren't people always happy at Christmas?

Ben squeezed under the bottom of the door to get out of the cold. He slowly and carefully headed toward the chair and hid in the shadow of it's leg.

Ben watched the old man fold his arms on the table, lay his head down and nod off to sleep.

He felt sorry for the sad old man. What could a mouse do to make him happy? Ben thought and thought. Studying the room, he spotted a bare Christmas tree leaning against a stone fireplace.

I've got it! I'll decorate the old man's tree, maybe that might cheer him up.

A wooden box was next to the tree filled with all sorts of Christmas treasures: painted ornaments, silver bells, strung popcorn and yellowed candles. It was no easy task for such a small mouse, to bring the decorations one by one from the box, up the tree, across the limbs — to hang each ornament and string the popcorn just right. Ben knew he had to work fast before the old man woke up.

As the last ornament was carefully placed, he realized his first wish had come true — he decorated a Christmas tree!

Ben rubbed his eyes with his tiny fists. A big yawn and warm, pinkish ears told him he needed a nap. Though it had been fun, he was tired from all his hard work. He climbed down the tree and pulled himself up into a scuffed boot, near the cozy, warm fireplace. Soon he was fast asleep.

Later that evening, the old man woke up to a dazzling bright light dancing in the room. Amazed, he wondered who had decorated his Christmas tree so beautifully.

As he circled around, admiring the tree, he noticed something in his right boot. He picked it up, and what do you think he found? A wee mouse, fast asleep. He couldn't believe it — A MOUSE!

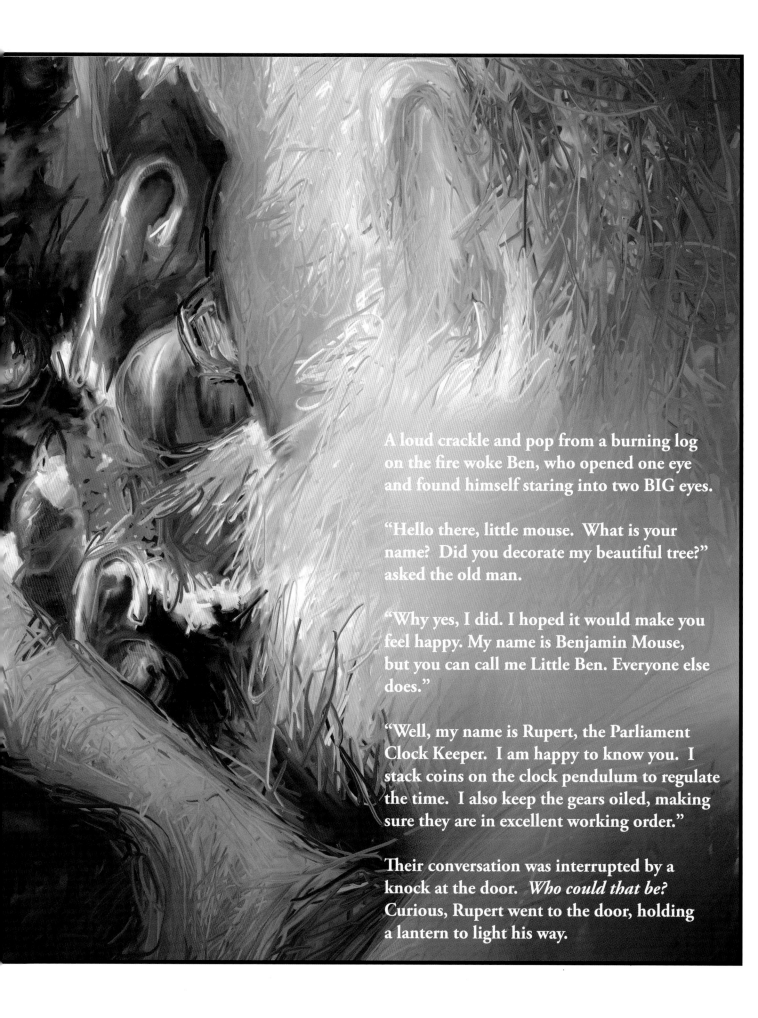

A loud crackle and pop from a burning log on the fire woke Ben, who opened one eye and found himself staring into two BIG eyes.

"Hello there, little mouse. What is your name? Did you decorate my beautiful tree?" asked the old man.

"Why yes, I did. I hoped it would make you feel happy. My name is Benjamin Mouse, but you can call me Little Ben. Everyone else does."

"Well, my name is Rupert, the Parliament Clock Keeper. I am happy to know you. I stack coins on the clock pendulum to regulate the time. I also keep the gears oiled, making sure they are in excellent working order."

Their conversation was interrupted by a knock at the door. *Who could that be?* Curious, Rupert went to the door, holding a lantern to light his way.

The Royal Messenger stood at the door and exclaimed, "The snowstorm is getting worse! It is so icy, it's blinding! Her Majesty is worried! She is relying on the clock tower bell to ring out at midnight, sounding the beginning of Christmas for all of London."

Every year without fail, the clock tower bell guides Father Christmas to London, especially during bad weather. Alarmed by the messenger's news, Rupert reached into his pocket for his watch — but it wasn't there. Little Ben had already taken it. Hanging from the lantern, Ben opened the pocket watch so Rupert could read the time better.

"Oh, no! It's midnight and the clock has not rung! Father Christmas won't hear the tower bell and will surely miss London!" Rupert shouted in a panic, "Ben, quick, hold on tight to the lantern. We haven't a moment to lose!"

They raced up the winding stairs toward the top of the clock tower to see why the bell hadn't rung.

Ice had formed on the clock hands, jamming the clock — the bell could not ring!

Little Ben knew what he had to do. He jumped off Rupert's lantern and dashed outside.

Racing after Ben, Rupert reached the window and looked outside at the clock's face. He gasped in shock, seeing his little friend slowly edging across it's massive bronze hands.

"Little Ben! Little Ben! Hold on tight, it is slippery, don't look down!" shouted Rupert.

Ben was so cold, he could hardly keep his teeth from chattering. Yet with determination, he began to gnaw at the ice that had frozen and stopped the clock. His strong front teeth broke through the binding ice; the clock hands shuddered and began to move. The tower bell boldly rang out.

The rest happened so suddenly! The jolt from the moving hands made Little Ben lose his grip and fall, down, down, down to the street below. Rupert heard a tiny voice crying out — fading into the snowy fog.

Rupert was heartbroken. His eyes filled with tears, thinking he had lost his new little friend who had tried so bravely to help save Christmas. As Rupert wiped his teary eyes, a sudden gust of wind blew through the clock tower window. A red flash of light warmed the icy air.
How strange! thought Rupert.

Moments later, Rupert felt something touch his shirtsleeve.

"Hey, Rupert!" a wee voice squeaked. "Rupert! Rupert! It's me, Little Ben!"

Rupert could not believe his eyes or his ears. Ben was all right — but how?

"You won't believe it! You just won't believe it, Rupert! It was like a dream, but it wasn't a dream. Guess what happened! Guess! Guess! I was saved by none other than — FATHER CHRISTMAS! My wish came true!" squeaked Little Ben.

Little Ben continued to tell Rupert the amazing story, "The clock hands were so slippery, I couldn't hold on when they began to move. I fell. It was hard to see in all that snow. The wind picked me up, blew me all about, and dropped me into the fold of his soft, furry, red hat!"

Excitedly, Ben talked faster and faster, "Father Christmas couldn't find London in the storm. He heard the clock bell ring just in time! He said I was very brave and thanked me for helping him find his way. That made me feel very special!"

"Then in a flash, I was back at the clock tower and here I am. Isn't it wonderful, Rupert? I actually met Father Christmas!" said Little Ben, jumping with glee.

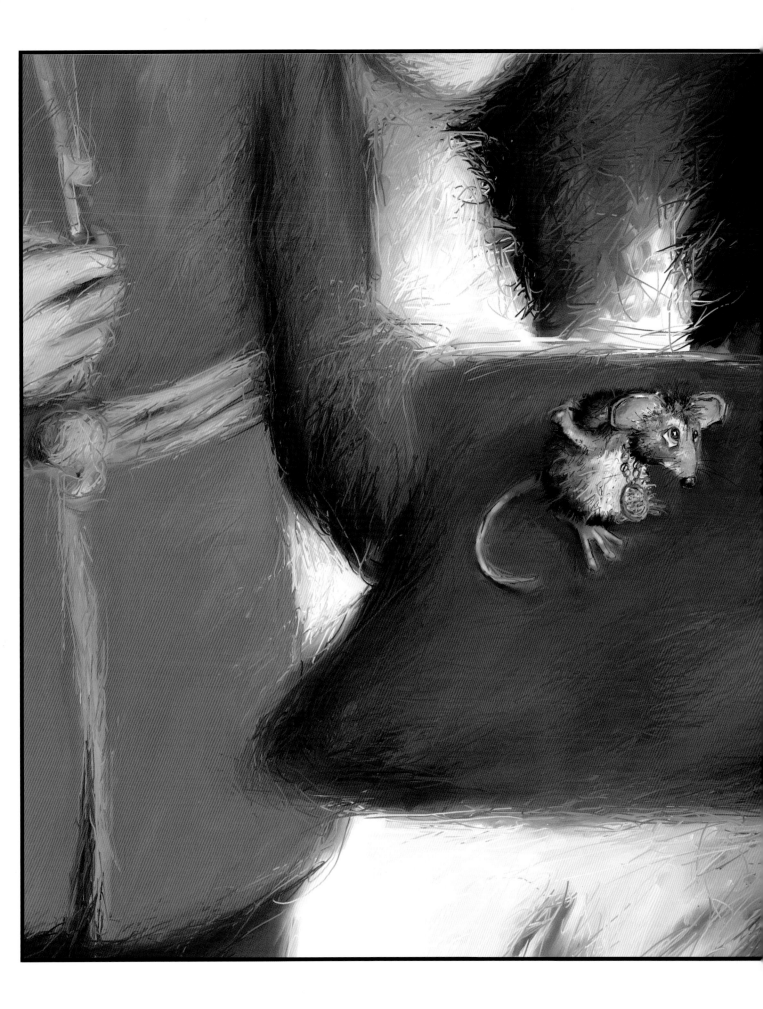

The news of how a little mouse risked his life to save Christmas traveled throughout London, even the Queen heard about it!

She also learned that it was Little Ben's dream for everyone to celebrate Christmas, including the mice. Therefore, the Queen proclaimed, "No mouse in London shall be too busy gathering food to celebrate the holidays. I would ask that each family in London put out minced pie, candy and cheese to feed the mice. From this day forward, I hope everyone will have time to celebrate Christmas — including mice!"

"Little Ben, you have done such a heroic BIG deed for London," the Queen exclaimed. She paused as the clock bell rang out in celebration, "We are forever grateful. From now on, we will call you — BIG BEN!"

The Queen's new name for Ben quickly spread all over London; everyone agreed it was a fitting title. Londoners would recall Big Ben and his bravery whenever the tower bell was heard.

To this day, mice proudly tell the story of how one small mouse saved Christmas and why the Parliament Clock Tower is now know as "Big Ben."

On special occasions, I proudly wear Her Majesty's gold medal and remember that
magical day, years ago, when I decorated my first Christmas tree,
met my long-time friend, Rupert and you know who, Father Christmas.

The End!